Scaredy-cat, Splat!

HarperCollins *Children's Books*

Rob Scotton

"MUM!" cried Splat. "There's a scary spider on my pumpkin! He's small and hairy with really funny eyes."

Splat's voice wobbled with worry.

"But you're small and hairy with really funny eyes," said his mum.

Splat thought for a moment.
"But I haven't got eight legs," he replied.
"If you had, maybe you'd be a scary spider too?" teased his mum.
Splat made a scary-spider face.

Splat's mum caught the spider under a glass jar. Splat looked closely at the spider. It didn't look so scary now that it was trapped.

"Can I take the spider to school for Halloween?" asked Splat.
"We've all made pumpkin heads and everyone is dressing up in costumes and Mrs Wimpydimple is going to tell a ghost story and there's a prize for the scariest cat and I want to be the scariest cat!
"So please can I take the spider to school... P-L-E-A-S-E?" he added without taking a breath.
"Okay," said his mum.

"Where's your Halloween costume?" asked his mum.
Splat pulled a broom from the cupboard and sat astride it.

"Aha! Look at me. I'm a scary witch's cat," cried Splat, racing around the kitchen.
"You certainly are scary," said his mum.

Then disaster struck.
Splat tripped over his tail and with a CRACK!
the broom handle snapped in two.

His scary witch's cat costume was ruined.

"Now I've got nothing to wear!" Splat groaned.
Even Seymour couldn't console him.

Splat's mum had an idea.
She stuffed some old socks with scrunched-up
newspaper and tied them to Splat with string.
"There!" she said.

Splat looked in the mirror and jumped back with a squeal. "Ohhh... I scared myself," he said.

He looked again and this time he smiled.
"Look at me!" he cried, waving his sock legs.
"I'm a big, scary sock spider."

Splat placed his pumpkin and spider on his wagon and set off to school.

On the way, he met Spike dressed as a mummy
and Plank dressed as a skeleton.

"They're pretty scary," said Splat.
Seymour nodded and trembled a little.

"But I'm scarier," said Splat.
Splat made his scariest spider face and growled.

Grrrrrrr.

Spike and Plank didn't even blink.

Instead...

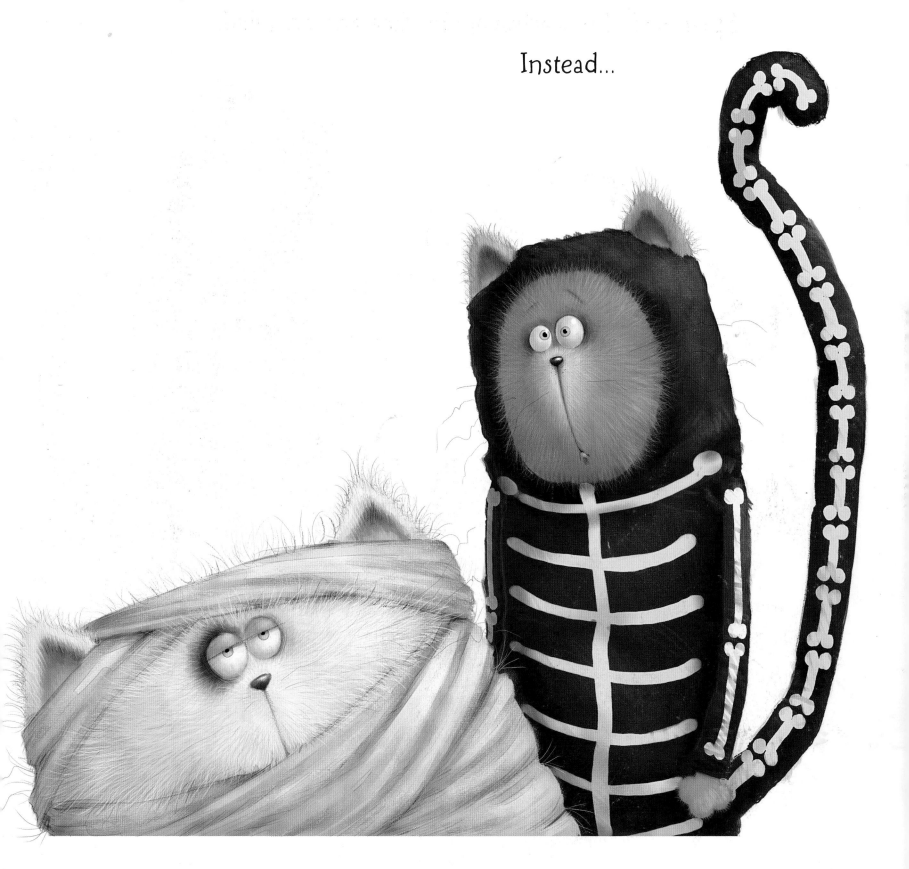

"BOO!" cried Spike.

"BOO!"

cried Plank.

Splat yelped and jumped high in the air...

and landed in a heap.

"Aww," Splat sighed. "Spike and Plank are both scarier than me."
Seymour nodded and trembled a little bit more.
"I'll never win the prize for scariest cat," said Splat.

The sock spider, the skeleton and the mummy
continued on their way to school.

In class, everyone showed their pumpkin heads.

Splat's pumpkin made everyone laugh.

"Awww," Splat sighed. "I'll never win the prize for scariest cat."

Seymour shook his head.

Everyone placed torches in their pumpkins and Mrs Wimpydimple turned down the lights and whispered in her best ghost-story voice.

"In the dark, dark wood there's a dark, dark house.

In the dark, dark house there's a dark, dark room.

In the dark, dark room there's a dark, dark box...

and in the dark, dark box there's... a...

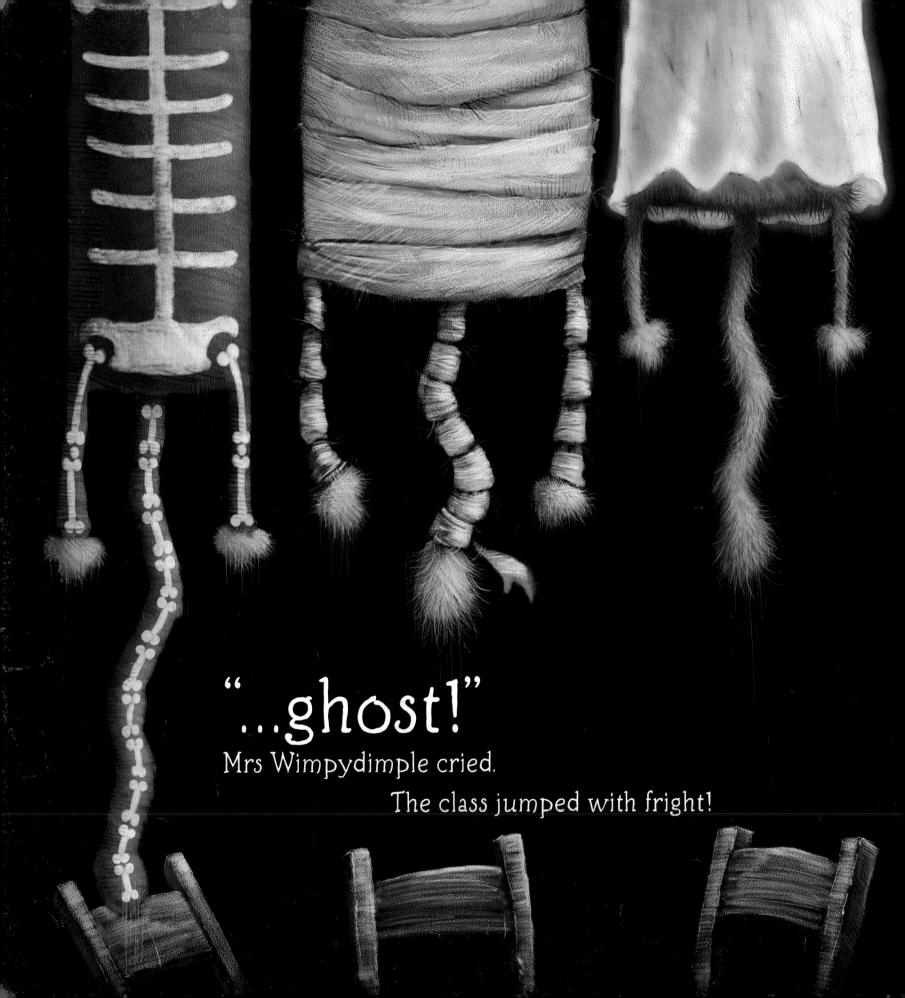

"...ghost!"
Mrs Wimpydimple cried.
The class jumped with fright!

Splat was so startled, his tail whipped around and sent his pumpkin spinning through the air.
And what goes up must come down.

SPLAT!

Unable to see anything, Splat stumbled around the classroom.

Everyone shrieked as the pumpkin head glared
at them and made strange whoo-whoo-ing noises.

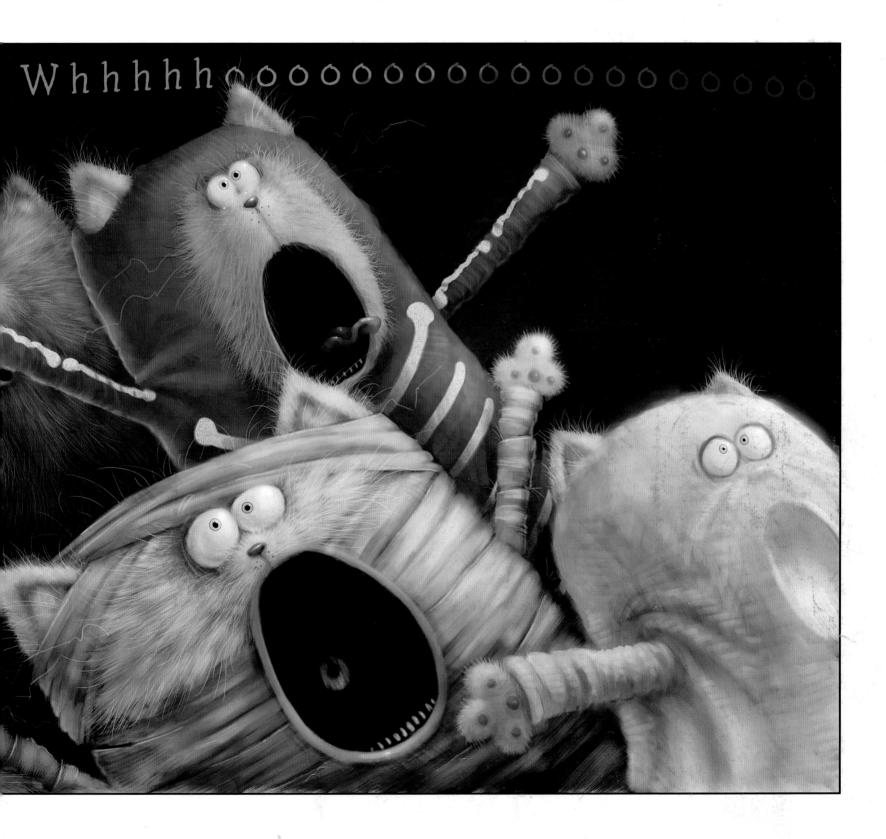

Mrs Wimpydimple turned on the lights and lifted up the wayward pumpkin.

The shrieking turned to laughter as Splat fell out.

"Calm down, calm down," hushed Mrs Wimpydimple. "Now, class, who should win the prize for being the scariest cat?"